Russell Morris
Illustrations by Billie Morris

McGregor &
The Embeebee Forest

Bumblebee Books
London

BUMBLEBEE PAPERBACK EDITION

Copyright © Russell Morris 2022
Illustrations by Billie Morris

A CIP catalogue record for this title is
available from the British Library.

ISBN: 978-1-83934-647-7

Bumblebee Books is an imprint of
Olympia Publishers.

First Published in 2022

Bumblebee Books
Tallis House
2 Tallis Street
London
EC4Y 0AB

Printed in Great Britain

www.olympiapublishers.com

Dedication

This book wouldn't exist without Anni & Harry
and the team at MBB.

Mᵗ MANN

The Beginning

This story starts in a magical place called The Embeebee Forest. It was no normal forest. And no one knew how it came about, it was just special.

The Embeebee Forest was situated at the base of a large mountain called Mount Mann and circled by a wide horseshoe-shaped lake, which made it nearly an island and very difficult to access. The mountain resembled the head and shoulders of a giant bearded man rising out of the earth; the lake resembled his giant arms, which enclosed the forest as his own.

At the front of the forest, there was a large tree that had fallen across the narrowest part of the lake, connecting the forest to the outside world. Beyond this crossing was a long protective wall of thick, prickly shrubs and bushes concealing the lake and beyond this, sprawling fields of luscious long grass for as far as the eye could see.

Mount Mann was steep and craggy, with the thick bush making up his beard and dark caves resembling his eyes and nose.

Directly above Mount Mann, there was a lone silver star that would shine with extraordinary intensity. Even during the day you could see it glimmering, as if it was competing with the afternoon sun. The star shone directly onto an open, grassed area in the forest some called 'The Green'. It was like a giant spotlight shining on the main arena at a circus. Legend would say The Embeebee Star had something to do with the strange happenings in the forest.

The Embeebee Forest was home to many different animals

from different parts of the world, and strangely enough, they could all talk to one another. In another place, in another life, some of them would have seen the others not as friends, but as their lunch. But in The Embeebee Forest, they all seemed to get along.

Chapter 1

During the day, The Embeebee Forest was always bathed in sunshine. The surrounding lake and thick, prickly shrubs and bushes made all the animals inside feel safe from potential intruders.

On the other side of the protective wall of vegetation, the grassy field was deemed part of the outside world and therefore seen as a place to avoid. Most of the animals from The Embeebee Forest had never ventured outside before.

Beyond the field was a small, thatch-roofed cottage with a freshly painted picket fence and a manicured vegetable garden that was the pride and joy of Old Man Calahan and his wife, Harriet.

CALAHAN'S COTTAGE

They would spend hours in their garden, looking after their precious tomatoes, carrots, potatoes, silverbeet and more.

The Calahan's didn't have any children, but they were kept company by their large and friendly Labrador dog called McGregor.

McGregor was very adventurous and always wanted to explore. He often ate too much and sometimes tried to bury his bones in the veggie garden, much to the annoyance of Old Man Calahan.

"Stop digging holes in my garden, you silly dog," Calahan would grumble.

McGregor was such a glutton he once ate a possum whole!

His favourite pastime was to run through the tall grass in the surrounding fields and head straight towards the thicket concealing the forest, but old man Calahan would never let McGregor venture any further.

"Don't you even think about it," Calahan would snap. McGregor had an old soul and knew there was something special to be discovered out there towards the giant mountain. One day, he knew he would get the chance to check it out. What McGregor didn't know was what awaited him there.

Chapter 2

On one particular day, McGregor was doing what he normally would, fossicking for something to eat and looking for some way to satisfy his hunger. Sometimes, McGregor thought his stomach was like a bottomless pit.

"I'm starving," he was always telling himself.

His keen nose led him through the surrounding fields and in the direction of the craggy mountain, towards the thick line of prickly bushes protecting the surrounding lake. He had been down this path before, but Old Man Calahan would always deliver a short and sharp whistle to order him back to the cottage. This time, however, Calahan was distracted in his veggie garden, allowing the adventurous dog to wander out of sight.

OLD MAN CALAHAN

McGregor had picked up an unfamiliar scent. He wasn't sure if it was food, but it certainly made him curious. He followed it with blind enthusiasm. Many animals would exercise caution, but not McGregor—he was too excitable, and maybe a bit silly.

Not far from McGregor, an inquisitive young squirrel was also busy fossicking for her dinner. Squizzle was an energetic young squirrel with a beautiful silky fur coat.

She lived in the forest with a mixture of animals. She never stopped working, whether it be sorting her food provisions or managing other issues in the forest.

Everything needed to be organised and planned or she would get upset. In fact, it was her curiosity to know every detail about everyone and everything in the forest that would soon change her life.

She'd been busily collecting nuts all afternoon, and was now washing them by the lake's edge. Earlier in the day, she'd been invited by her close friend, Franky the fox, to sneak out to the open field beyond the lake, to chat and gossip about goings-on in the forest. Squizzle knew it was a no-go to go out past the lake, but was excited by the idea nonetheless.

SQUiZZLe

I wonder what Franky wants to share with me today, she thought.

Franky was a street-smart silver fox who had lived a busy life and had many stories to tell. He wasn't always silver—in his youth, he had sported a strawberry blonde mane and bushy tail, and had bounded around like he was the 'ant's pants'. Now he was content to befriend all the animals in the forest and pass on any wisdom he could.

BYRON

Franky's group of friends called themselves 'The Team', led by his mentor, a good friend and big brown bear named Byron.

"Hey, Squiz, how about we have some fun and take off for a run around in the long grass?" Franky would cheekily suggest. "We need to talk about something and I don't want anyone to hear us."

They did this quite often, as many of The Team had the keenest ears and could hear Franky and Squizzle chattering from a long distance. It didn't matter that team member Brenda could always see them out on the field, they just wanted to be out of earshot.

BRENDA

Brenda was a tough old barn owl, appointed to watch over the entrance to the forest. She was crafty and her sharp eyesight allowed her to warn The Team of any potential intruders to the forest. Brenda liked to know everything that was going on in the forest. Byron called

Brenda their very own 'watch bird'. She loved this nickname.

Though she was ordinarily stern, Brenda had a soft spot for Franky, and would occasionally let him and Squizzle cross the tree-trunk to the outside field.

FRANKY

"Just make sure you stay in my line of sight," Brenda would order.

Meanwhile, just beyond the grassy field, McGregor's nose had started to tingle. The scent was getting stronger and it had now led him to the edge of a prickly thicket. He was determined to satisfy his curiosity and carefully manoeuvred his way through the sharp thorns. Though the thorns stung his paws, nothing could come between McGregor's nose and an interesting smell. Was it food? Something else? Finally, he reached the end of the prickly path, and poked his head out of the bushes. He could hardly believe his eyes! There it was, The Embeebee Forest.

Chapter 3

In the spring, The Embeebee Forest was a beautiful place. The sunshine had melted the last of the winter snow and the flowers were starting to bloom. The lake was a turquoise blue and on this particular day, you could see the image of the giant mountain and forest reflected on its surface. McGregor's eyes popped out of his head and his large pink tongue dangled from his mouth in shock.

Normally nothing would surprise McGregor, but what he could see was extraordinary. He knew the mountain and forest existed, they were enormous, you couldn't miss them—but he had never been allowed to see them up close. The expansive lake, the giant fallen tree-trunk. The thick forest of tall trees, ferns, bushes and flowers. It was quite spectacular.

"Wow, I didn't know the forest looked like that," McGregor growled to himself.

Squizzle was completing her washing duties at the lake's edge when she was startled by an unfamiliar growling and gruffling noise.

"Who are you?" McGregor barked.

Squizzle looked up to see a very strange-looking animal staring back at her, and immediately she went into 'fight or flight' mode. She chose the latter. She tried to take off but she panicked, lost her footing and slipped right into the lake.

Squirrels weren't the best swimmers at the best of times, and Squizzle was no exception. She was already starting to sink. McGregor was in shock, but his instincts kicked in quickly, he leapt into the lake after the stranger squirrel, scooped her up in his mouth like a father would his puppies, and swam to the other side of the lake, towards the forest. McGregor was a strong swimmer, not to mention filled with adrenaline from his surprise encounter.

By now, Brenda was hooting and squawking alarm bells at the top of her lungs. Hearing Brenda's alarm, Franky burst forth from the forest's edge, only to see a large animal emerging from the lake with his best friend in his mouth.

Franky pounced on McGregor's back, causing him to release the startled squirrel from his toothy grip. Squizzle dropped with a thud to the ground. The courageous fox bit and scratched at the dangerous intruder, the sound of their scuffle catching the attention of many of the other forest animals. They cheered Franky on, gnashing their teeth, hissing, growling, squawking, hooting, yelping. At that point, Squizzle seemed to have recovered from her shock and the water she'd swallowed, and got her senses back.

"Franky, get off him! Get off!" she squealed at the top of her voice. She tried to jump between the fighting parties.

Franky was reluctant, this strange animal had tried to eat his best friend! But he always listened to Squizzle. He took a few steps back from McGregor, but he refused to take his eyes off the dog for even a second.

Byron and the rest of The Team had by then joined Franky and Squizzle at the lake, and they had McGregor surrounded. There would be no escape now for the intruder.

McGregor stood up to vigorously shake all the lake water from his thick chocolate coat. He was now staring at a giant bear, an agitated wolf, a sleek black panther, a scowling owl and a very serious-looking raven. He was in shock, what had just happened? Could these strange, talking animals living in the forest be real? It was all a bit much for McGregor.

What have I got myself into here? he thought to himself. *"And how am I going to get myself out of it?"*

Chapter 4

Franky quickly checked Squizzle to see if she was alright; luckily, she was fine. All she wanted was to reassure her animal friends, The Team, that this strange creature had saved her life.

"I was finishing up at the lake and he gave me such a fright I slipped right in the water," she told them, "but then he grabbed me and saved my life."

McGregor was still in shock, he could understand every word the feisty squirrel was saying! While he could understand other dogs, he'd never been able to speak to any other kind of animal before. The Embeebee Forest had now cast its magic onto the curious brown dog.

The Team comprised a variety of animals that McGregor had never come across before.

There was Byron, a big, strong brown bear and the leader of The Team. He slept in a large cave at the base of the mountain, guarding over the forest. Everyone felt safe with Byron around.

In his typical manner, he calmly stepped forward and spoke. "Well, who or what are you, then?" Byron said.

McGregor was still shaken by the talking squirrel and now he was in the presence of a talking bear!

McGregor explained that he was from the other side of the lake and lived in a cottage beyond the grassy field and prickly thorns. The Team knew of the cottage, the serious-looking Raven, whose name was Poppy, had flown out that way and described it to them but they had never ventured out that far before.

He told them of Old Man Calahan and Harriet, the vegetable garden they were both so proud of, and how he had picked up the scent of Franky and Squizzle from the field. This did not please Byron and caused an upset amongst the rest of The Team as what had they been doing outside the forest?

Franky and Squizzle apologised, but The Team were all much more interested in McGregor than the apologies of a wily old fox and an adventurous squirrel.

McGregor described for them what the world outside The Embeebee Forest looked like. He just liked the fact that he could now talk to and understand strange animals he had never even seen or heard of before.

By now, McGregor had earned some of The Team's trust and was invited to join them back at The Green to tell more of his stories about the strange world outside of the forest.

But there was one cautious member of The Team who wasn't ready to trust an uninvited visitor to the forest. That was the wolf, Rhys. That was just his nature.

Rhys was second in charge to Byron and very protective of the forest and The Team. The other animals were scared he was going to eat them, and if it wasn't for Byron he might just have done so. He had been there for a long time and knew the forest and its goings-on like the back of his paw.

As they all walked back towards The Green, Rhys had a quick chance to whisper in Byron's ear.

"What do you think of the fast-talking dog? I don't know about you, but I don't trust him," said Rhys.

"Give him a chance," Byron replied. "Let's not judge him so quickly."

Chapter 5

Old Man Calahan was getting worried. The sun was setting and McGregor was nowhere to be seen.

He had been distracted in his garden for several hours, but he had a feeling that something was wrong, so he set out searching for McGregor late in the afternoon. After many hours of whistling and calling out McGregor's name, he could now only hope he was alright.

"Where could he be?" Calahan said to Harriet. "Has he run away? How could he do that to us? Or what if he's hurt and he can't get to us?" Calahan went on and on.

Meanwhile, the mischievous young dog was having a wonderful time deep in The Embeebee Forest sharing stories with a bunch of new friends, at least, that's how he felt.

Like Rhys, the black panther Zeka was also wary of the intruder at first. While they didn't always see eye to eye, they both agreed that McGregor's discovery of their home was a serious concern. Plus, they didn't like that Franky and Squizzle had broken The Team's rules.

Squizzle was quite taken by McGregor's tales of the unfamiliar land outside the forest, of a cottage and a town with many buildings, and two-legged creatures, humans, he called them, that fed him and looked after him.

"I get fed and looked after by my keepers, the old man and lady," McGregor had boasted.

Back at home, Harriet was flustered trying to deal with two major issues, first the disappearance of her beloved McGregor, and now the panicked behaviour of her husband.

Calahan had turned to pacing the cottage, muttering things under his breath about the 'stupid dog' and 'there won't be a next time'. He planned to lock McGregor up as soon as he got home as punishment.

"If he's gone down to that forest, he's in big trouble," Calahan told Harriet.

Just as the sun began to drop behind the horizon, it dawned on McGregor that he had been away from home a long time. He motioned politely to his new friends that he needed to go back to his cottage and keeper, and asked whether he could come back for a return visit.

Byron asked for a show of paws, wings, and feet for a vote, a majority agreed that McGregor could come back. This gave McGregor a warm feeling inside, not only had he made new friends, but they were much more interesting than the local dogs in town, who only ever wanted to sniff each other and chase cats.

Byron asked Brenda if she would escort McGregor back to the tree-trunk to cross the lake, as she had the best night vision. Squizzle also volunteered to help, as she felt indebted to McGregor for saving her life.

It was well after dinner time when McGregor finally bounded up to the cottage gate, barking excitedly as if to say, "I'm home!"

Old Man Calahan jumped up out of his favourite armchair and raced to the door, nearly tripping on the rug's edge in all his excitement.

Chapter 6

Calahan swung the front door open so fast it thudded against the cottage wall, and before he could say one word, McGregor had leapt from the first step of the landing into Calahan's arms, knocking him backward into the living room. The full weight of an overly nourished McGregor sent the old man firmly onto his backside, startling Harriet, who had been eagerly waiting for McGregor's return beside the open fireplace.

"Oh my god, oh my god," was all Old Man Calahan could say.

McGregor continued to lick Calahan's face until the old man wrestled him away with all his strength. Old Man Calahan could barely control himself, he was so angry that McGregor had stayed away for so long and put him and Harriet through such hell. He was torn between relief and anger, but as usual, Calahan's anger prevailed.

"Where have you been, you stupid dog?" he shouted.

McGregor was happy to be back home with his family, but he had underestimated the consequences of his adventure. But the old man let McGregor know exactly what he and Harriet had been through—and he didn't hold back.

"Right," Calahan said, "you're not going anywhere for a while, young man."

All McGregor's licking and slobbering affection could not dissuade Old Man Calahan from grounding McGregor from leaving the house. McGregor was delivered a criminal punishment: imprisonment in the cottage, so he couldn't continue his exciting adventure.

For how long, he did not know. He could only hope that someday, he'd see his friends from The Embeebee Forest again.

Chapter 7

Squizzle woke the next day with a spring in her step and a sparkle in her eye. She had had a life-changing moment with a strange creature, and now she had a whole new lease on life. There was so much more beyond the bounds of their forest! She couldn't wait to meet McGregor again and hear more about the outside world.

"Today is a great day," declared Squizzle.

Franky was the opposite—he'd woken up on the wrong side of the den. He, too, had had a life-changing moment, only he wasn't as excited about it as Squizzle. McGregor had rocked his world.

"What's so good about it?" Franky said. "All the dog did was get us in trouble, he blabbed to everyone about how he caught our scent outside the forest. Byron and Rhys are not happy with us."

The strange dog had come along and upset the whole make-up of the forest and taken all the attention away from the ego-driven Franky. In Franky's mind, McGregor was just an annoying disruption.

In times of uncertainty, Franky liked to go and seek the advice of Zeka, the young, powerful black panther. Not everyone liked Zeka. She was a loner and would get frustrated and angry at times at the way things happened in the forest. But Franky found her a very good judge of character, and a trusted friend.

"What do you make of McGregor, the dog we all met yesterday?" asked Franky.

Zeka said she had initially thought McGregor could be trouble, but she'd soon endeared to him. "I like him," she told Franky. "Although he's still a stranger, we'll need to watch him."

Franky took a deep breath and reflected on Zeka's advice. He decided to wait and see how things panned out before he judged McGregor. It would turn out to be a good decision.

Chapter 8

It had been a while since they had seen McGregor, which surprised Franky and Squizzle a little. They had almost all been enthralled by the dog's stories of the strange outside world and the animals he called 'humans'. Though Franky had been wary at first, he was now quite excited by the prospect of finding out more about the outside world as well.

"Hey, Squiz," Franky said to the inquisitive squirrel, "aren't you curious to find out more about the outside world and those 'humans' McGregor talked about?"

"Sure am," Squizzle replied right away.

Franky suggested that they go and find McGregor and invite him back for another storytelling session. But since that fateful day, both Byron and Rhys had insisted that if Franky and Squizzle were ever caught venturing outside again, the consequences would be severe. Brenda wouldn't let them out again either.

"But, if we got caught leaving the forest, we could become entree and main course for Rhys's next meal," Squizzle said.

"Don't be silly, that will never happen," Franky reassured her.

Although it was easy for Brenda and Poppy to venture out beyond the forest as they could fly, it was a no-go for the rest of The Team.

Poppy was a loyal and reliable raven, but also very mysterious, she flew in and out of the forest at will, but no one ever knew where she went or what she was up to. When questioned where she'd been, she would always answer with another question.

"Where do you think I've been?" she'd respond.

But no one knew what to say, as the world beyond the forest was a mystery to all the other animals.

Getting past Brenda and Poppy without being seen was going to be a tough task. Franky and Squizzle both knew that Brenda had keen eyes and she would be perched in the large tree overlooking the entrance to the lake. Poppy would be skimming along the forest tree tops pretending to mind her own business, but really keeping a sharp eye on the animals below her.

POPPY

Franky and Squizzle put their heads together to devise a plan. Early in the morning, Brenda would always get hungry and take a break from guarding the forest to hunt for her breakfast. Even when she got back, her and Poppy's attention would be focused on the tree-trunk, as it seemed that was the only way across the lake.

"I've got an idea," Franky piped up. "How about we swim across?"

Squizzle's eyes grew wide with alarm. "Swim?!"

Chapter 9

That same morning, Byron had decided it was time to call a team meeting on The Green. Though the intruding McGregor was long gone, some members of The Team had grown worried that the forest wasn't secure enough, and Rhys had been badgering him to make sure there were serious consequences for anyone who broke The Team's rules.

Byron caught Brenda as she was returning from her hunt for breakfast. "Send out a message that we're having an urgent team meeting on The Green," Byron ordered.

Brenda flew with absolute grace and her hooting call could be heard across the forest. It didn't take long for The Team to get the message and head towards The Green. Many of the animals were already up and about, as the excitement earlier that week had left them unable to sleep.

The Embeebee Star shone through a gap in the clouds onto The Green as The Team gathered at their meeting place. Byron and Rhys were standing on a rock ledge overlooking them all, but something just wasn't quite right.

Brenda was busy ushering the animals into the clearing, Zeka was singing quietly to herself as she slinked through the star's spotlight onto the grassy section of The Green. They had all arrived except Franky and Squizzle. Rhys was annoyed, he was keen to get discussions underway right away, to make clear the consequences for any future rule breaker.

"Where are Franky and Squizzle?" asked Rhys. The animals all looked around at one another, but nobody responded. Nobody had seen the fox and squirrel all morning.

"Brenda, fly around again and see if you can spot them," ordered Byron.

They were nowhere to be found.

Chapter 10

"You know what happened last time I went swimming!" Squizzle reminded Franky. "It's a long way and how will we get past Poppy and Brenda without being spotted splashing in the water?"

Franky shared his idea with Squizzle, and they decided to go ahead with it.

A short distance around from the tree-trunk was a wide section of the lake that was obscured from the watch birds. It was a very long stretch of water to the other side. Although older, Franky was still quite fit and it was decided that Squizzle would ride on the back of his neck while he carefully and quietly fox-paddled across.

Like clockwork, Brenda had instructed Poppy to take watch as she went on her search for breakfast. Franky and Squizzle were hiding in thick grass a short distance away, ready for their long swim. Stealthily, Franky slid into the water and invited Squizzle to jump onto his back. She gripped his neck with her claws, there wasn't much fur there, so her claws dug in, making for an irritating swim across the large stretch of water.

Franky shuddered as the cold water lapped his underbelly. "Make sure you hold on tightly, just as we planned," he instructed his friend.

Frantically he paddled through the cold and calm water, careful not to create any splashing, which would draw the attention of Poppy and see the quick return of Brenda to her perch. Franky had to move quickly or Poppy would have easily spotted a swimming fox carrying a small squirrel across the lake. Though he was swimming as fast as he could, they had so far to go, it felt like he'd been swimming for an eternity.

"Are you okay?" Squizzle checked in every now and then.

"I'm good. Don't you worry about me, you just hold on and keep watch," Franky replied.

With the lake's edge finally only a short distance away, they had almost made a perfect getaway when Squizzle caught a glimpse of a black object skimming across the sky towards them. It was Poppy. She was on a reconnaissance fly-over, looking for the missing Team Members.

"Franky, I can see Poppy!" warned Squizzle.

Thinking quickly, Franky took a duck dive, much to the surprise of the bareback-riding squirrel. They both went under the water, and stayed under for what seemed like ages. Franky tried desperately to paddle under the water towards the muddy slope on the edge of the lake. His lungs were about to burst, as were Squizzle's who was still in shock from the surprise underwater adventure.

When he couldn't take it anymore, Franky's nose pierced the water's surface and he let out a desperate gasp for air. They'd made it to the lake's edge! Exhausted, Franky slid on his belly across the muddy slope, through the prickly scrub and into the long grass, settling momentarily for a much-needed rest. In all the confusion, he had forgotten about Squizzle on his back. She had rolled off him and into the grass, and was now lying with her legs and arms in the air, motionless.

"Oh no," Franky said under his breath. "What have I done?"

Chapter 11

For what felt like forever, McGregor had been sitting on the side table under the window in the main living room, staring at the distant silhouette of Mount Mann. The jagged cliff-face looked to him like Calahan's, and the treetops of the forest under his bearded face swayed in the breeze, as though they were tickling his chin.

Calahan had locked all the doors, and would only let McGregor out every now and then for a relief stop. He even had a rope tied around the gate to prevent the naughty Labrador getting out.

Old Man Calahan was no dill. He was certain that McGregor had gone to the forest; he could see the dog staring out the window for hours at a time with his nose pointed squarely in the direction of the craggy old mountain. McGregor could only sigh and whimper, wondering when he might be allowed outside again to continue his adventure.

"You can keep dreaming, McGregor, but you ain't goin' nowhere," the old man would say to his dog.

Calahan had a feeling there was something unusual about that forest. In the past he had heard strange noises coming from its direction. He had never ventured over there, and never intended to. The bush and scrub was too thick to get through and he wasn't about to try.

Harriet and he had discussed what to do with McGregor, as they didn't want a repeat of him running away.

Calahan's heart couldn't handle the stress of it all.

"We can't keep him locked up forever," Harriet had said

to her husband.

"Let's at least keep him inside for a while until he settles down. We can take it in turns to walk him on the lead," Calahan had replied.

McGregor hated having a collar on and he hated being restricted to walking at a human's pace. But what could he do? He'd done the crime, now he'd have to do the time!

On that particular afternoon, Old Man Calahan had to go into town for some errands; as McGregor was under house arrest, Harriet would be prison warden for the rest of the day.

HARRIET

Chapter 12

Meanwhile, back at the forest, Byron and Rhys were in emergency mode. Poppy and Brenda had completed their fly-over looking for Franky and Squizzle with no success. The forest's fox and squirrel were missing. Byron and Rhys both suspected where they had probably gone.

"Well, Rhys, they've made my decision an easy one. Get a search party together and bring them back to the forest," Byron told his second in charge.

Rhys put his nose to work. He had a wonderful sense of smell, all he needed to do was find the scent and follow it. While Franky had his bushy trail to cover his tracks, he couldn't hide his and Squizzle's scents on their escape route across the lake.

"Zeka!" Rhys commanded. "You in?"

"Sure am," Zeka responded. "With your nose and my speed and athleticism, we're sure to catch them."

"Hey, Poppy, how about you fly ahead and give us the heads-up as to what we might expect from this 'outside world' McGregor talked so much about?" Rhys ordered.

"Aye aye, captain," said Poppy, and off she went.

Rhys and Zeka ventured down to the lake. In the meantime, Byron was questioning Brenda as to how she and Poppy could've missed the escapees travelling across the tree-trunk. Brenda was defensive and she assured Byron that she was an experienced watch bird, nothing would have escaped her keen eye.

"Poppy was covering my post while I had my breakfast,

she's absolutely certain they didn't go across the tree-trunk," Brenda said.

Rhys was already in search mode and since his nose was like a vacuum, it soon took in all the scents around him. Byron and the rest of the animals had full confidence in Rhys to sniff out the clues, and they knew both he and Zeka loved to hunt.

Rhys followed Franky and Squizzle's scents to where they entered the lake.

"They must have swum across," Rhys said. "It's a long way to the other side, I sure hope they didn't get into trouble on the way."

"Let's go and check it out," Zeka said.

The two of them bounded back to the tree-trunk and took off to the other side of the lake.

Chapter 13

Franky started to panic when he saw his best friend lying motionless in the long grass. He nudged Squizzle with his paw to try to draw some sort of response but got nothing.

"Squizzle… Squizzle… wake up, wake up!" Franky pleaded.

He had to think fast. What could he do?

With nothing to lose, the quick-thinking Franky placed his paw on Squizzle's chest and started pushing. He didn't really know what he was doing but he kept it going until all of a sudden Squizzle responded by spurting water straight into his face.

"Yes, it worked!" Franky proudly yelped.

Squizzle was curled up in the grass coughing and spluttering, getting her breath back, while Franky immediately shook the water from his face and went back into alert mode. They needed to keep moving.

"Are you okay?" Franky asked.

"Yes, but…" Squizzle responded. She looked a little woozy.

Franky cut her off. "Great. Now we need to focus."

"What happened?" Squizzle asked in a daze.

"Explain later. We have to keep moving," Franky said militantly.

There was no time to waste, it was already around midday, so they needed to find McGregor fast if they were going to get back to the forest before nightfall. They were in a strange land now, and neither of them liked the idea of spending the night out there.

From the stories McGregor had shared with them, they knew he lived in a cottage beyond the field. But the field they were in had very long grass, so they needed to work as a team.

Franky decided for Squizzle to jump onto his back again, she could stand on his head and be his eyes, like a squirrel periscope.

Squizzle loved this idea, especially as there was no water this time. She jumped on. From on top of Franky's head, she could see a vast distance above and beyond the grass line. Ahead of them Squizzle saw a grey, cloud-like substance cascading into the sky, which provided a beacon for her to follow.

"I think I can see something!" she yelled.

"Great," Franky replied. "Which way now?"

"That way!" Squizzle pointed squarely ahead.

Franky powered through the grass like a fox possessed. Squizzle had to hold on with all her strength or she would've been left behind. Eventually, they came to a clearing. Beyond this was a mud-brick structure with a wooden barrier protecting orderly rows of vegetation.

They looked just like the 'cottage', 'picket fence' and 'veggie garden' McGregor had described to The Team.

"This must be where he lives!" Squizzle said.

She jumped off Franky's back and they both scurried into the shadows at the side of the cottage. Their survival instincts had kicked in. They'd come out here with a job to do, and that was to find McGregor... but they hadn't talked about what they would do when they found him.

It was the early afternoon and McGregor was still in his bed when he was startled by movement outside. He had a feeling something was going on, so he jumped onto the side table and peered out his favourite window.

Chapter 14

Once across the lake, both Rhys and Zeka again put their noses to the test searching for a scent.

They needed to figure out exactly where Franky and Squizzle had come out of the water and in which direction to continue their search.

Their noses didn't let them down.

"Well, at least they made it across," Zeka sighed with relief.

"Yes, that was a long swim for a fox and squirrel to say the least," said Rhys.

Poppy had flown out ahead of them, but she couldn't spot Franky and Squizzle. It was up to Rhys and Zeka to use their skills to track down the two escapees.

Now that they'd picked up the scent again, Rhys and Zeka slowly and carefully negotiated their way through the thick prickly scrub that protected the lake. It was the type of stuff that would not have challenged a fox and small squirrel, but it certainly made hard work for the much larger wolf and panther. Out the other side of the scrub, Rhys and Zeka were able to pick up the pace and bounded effortlessly through the long grass towards the cottage.

Chapter 15

Harriet Calahan had been up for hours. She'd already cleaned up the old man's breakfast dishes and started on the laundry. She was now busily ringing the wet clothes of excess water, ready to hang them out on the clothesline to dry in the afternoon sun and warm spring breeze.

McGregor was up and about, pacing in the living room. Something was going on outside, he just knew it! He had a sensitive nose and instincts to boot, and he was getting more and more excited by the thought of what was about to transpire.

Franky and Squizzle had taken a pause and were crouched in the shadows of the Calahan cottage, trying to work out what to do next. It was only now beginning to truly dawn on them what they'd done, they'd left the safety of their forest for an unfamiliar place in search of a virtual stranger! Was it possible they'd made a mistake? Suddenly, they heard a loud bang. Harriet had slammed the back door and was heading towards the clothesline. From around the corner had emerged a strange-looking creature, walking on two legs. It walked across a small landing and started taking what looked like wet animal skins out of a basket to hang them on an oddly-shaped tree.

"What is that?!" Squizzle asked Franky, eyes wide in wonder.

"Maybe it's one of those humans McGregor had told us about," Franky said, awestruck too.

The two of them took off in the opposite direction to the other side of the cottage, hoping the unusual creature hadn't seen them.

Meanwhile, McGregor was going berserk inside the cottage, barking and barking, only to be shushed by an annoyed Harriet.

"Oh be quiet," she yelled at him from the clothesline. "What on Earth is wrong with you?"

Recognising the sound of McGregor's bark, the same sound that had sent her into the lake only a few days before! Franky and Squizzle turned to each other with a look of accomplishment. They had found McGregor—now they just needed to work out how to make contact with him.

Squizzle motioned for Franky to stand under the living room window, then for the third time that day, she jumped onto his back. She climbed onto his head and peered through the window into the cottage. She was met with the face of a big friendly Labrador staring straight back at her through the glass. McGregor was so excited he started licking the window! Squizzle laughed and had to dig her claws into Franky's skull to keep her balance.

"Owww! Take it easy," Franky growled. "What is it?"

"Franky, it's McGregor," Squizzle squealed. "He's right here!"

Chapter 16

Squizzle was still staring through the window at an excited McGregor when all of a sudden his expression changed to sheer panic.

"Take that, you meddling little critters!" Calahan shouted.

Old Man Calahan had crept up behind the unsuspecting pair and threw an old hessian sack over them. Caught in the sack, Franky and Squizzle went crashing into the landing outside the cottage. They were trapped and the more they fought, the more tangled they became.

McGregor jumped from the side table and went bounding towards the door, ramming into it with all his force but the door held its own and McGregor bounced right back onto the floor. He wasn't about to let his new friends be captured by Old Man Calahan. He could hear Squizzle's piercing squeals and Franky's low growls as Calahan struggled to heave the bag over his shoulder.

Harriet had, by this stage, dropped the washing in fright from the ruckus, and rushed around to see Old Man Calahan sneering with delight about his catch.

"Harriet, Harriet, I've caught a couple of sticky noses!" Calahan yelled proudly.

"What do you mean?" she replied.

"I got 'em, two of 'em! They're in the bag," he tried to explain.

"Two of what?" she asked, exasperated.

"A scummy fox and a vermin squirrel!" Calahan said.

"They were looking through the window, looking for food

I suspect. Or maybe they're from that forest and here to try to take McGregor away from us," he continued in desperation.

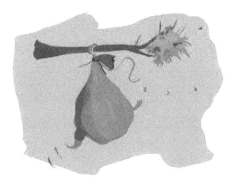 The old man strung the bag up on the highest tree branch he could reach, leaving the two captives trapped and scared. He was mindful of the cunning behaviour of his captured critters, he had a feeling they were smarter than they looked, especially if they were from that mysterious forest.

"I'll put 'em up here until we work out what to do with 'em," Calahan said villainously.

McGregor couldn't believe his eyes. Two animals he had only just met had come all this way to see him, and now they were in big trouble. Who knew what Calahan would do to them? McGregor wondered what he could do to help. Desperate times called for desperate measures. McGregor took off across the living room and leapt straight through his favourite window, the glass shattering around him. He dashed towards the tree where Franky and Squizzle were hanging, barking like crazy.

Chapter 17

Poppy had flown over the Calahan cottage and could see McGregor jumping and barking frantically at a strange object hanging from a tree. At closer inspection, she could hear the desperate cries of Franky and Squizzle coming from inside the hessian sack.

She had to inform Rhys and Zeka of her discovery right away, and tell them to get a move on. She took a sharp U-turn and soared back towards the advancing search party.

Total chaos ensued at the cottage. Old Man Calahan and Harriet were trying to put McGregor's lead on so they could lock him back up in the house, but he was too fast. He was running circles around the hanging sack and barking at the top of his lungs.

Franky and Squizzle had stopped struggling, and they could vaguely see McGregor and Calahan through a small hole in the hessian bag. They could also see two dark figures sprinting towards them, causing ripples through the long grass. Could it be—was that Rhys and Zeka, coming to their rescue?

McGregor also saw the rescuers running towards the cottage, and he took off to greet them. But Zeka was in total attack mode, leaping at him with all her might and knocking McGregor to the ground with a thud.

"Get out of my way," she hissed at McGregor. With superior reflexes, she flipped onto her feet and continued running towards the cottage.

Zeka reached the tree, launched herself onto the branch and started gnawing through the rope of the hessian bag.

"Franky, Squizzle, it's Zeka. Are you okay?" she said.

"I think so," Franky said.

"Just get us out of this thing!" Squizzle yelled.

Calahan and Harriet were in shock. A fox and squirrel had been one thing, but now a wolf and panther were on the loose at their house? Calahan dragged Harriet into the house, ran straight to the fireplace and he grabbed his old shotgun from its rack. He rushed back out onto the landing.

By then, Zeka had managed to free her friends from the bag and was retreating from the cottage to get them back to safety. All of a sudden, a piercing clap noise echoed in their ears. Old Man Calahan was pointing a long grey stick in their direction and it sure didn't look friendly. Rhys made a beeline for the armed Calahan and pounced on top of him. There was another loud clap as the gun fired straight into the air.

"Not today, old man," growled Rhys. He remembered the stories McGregor had told them about Calahan.

Then it was McGregor's turn to shine. Having recovered from Zeka's charge, he sprinted towards the attacking wolf, who by this stage had pinned Old Man Calahan to the ground. Calahan's gun was right in the middle of the kerfuffle and McGregor wasn't sure who was in more trouble.

McGregor threw his whole body weight into Rhys's ribs, causing him to gasp violently. They grappled on the ground. McGregor had to think quickly. He knew he was no match for the powerful wolf, but he needed to protect his keepers.

Calahan was distracted for a moment and Harriet had left the safety of the cottage to help him back to his feet. She hurried him back inside with her.

McGregor decided this was his chance. He pushed his snout in Rhys's ear and whispered: "Hey, I know I've only known you a short time, but you're going to have to trust me. Let's play a game," he proposed. "We pretend to fight a little, then you take off back into the forest with the others. I think we can save both of our skins." Instinctly, Rhys agreed.

They continued to wrestle a little and Rhys gave McGregor a nice smack with his powerful paw to the dog's snout. McGregor yelped and retaliated with a forceful bite. Rhys pretended to recoil in pain, then delivered a menacing and guttural growl and turned back towards his friends to run away. The startled McGregor had no choice but to pretend to chase but within an instant, the powerful wolf had already caught up with his friends. They rushed towards The Embeebee Forest, and McGregor was left staring stunned into the distance as the others disappeared into the long grass.

He found the old man and lady back inside the cottage, cowering in a corner of the kitchen. The sight of McGregor, their hero, had them both sigh with relief, which made McGregor immensely proud. He ran up to them both and licked their faces with delight.

What happened next was a surprise to everyone, Old Man Calahan started to cry. Not from the shock of being attacked by the wild animals from the forest, but from the sheer emotion of seeing his beloved McGregor risk his own life to protect him and his wife.

Harriet embraced the two with both arms. She too, was in total disbelief of McGregor's bravery, and even more so to see her stony-faced husband in such an emotional state. Never before had she seen him shed a tear. This was a very special moment for all of them.

"Oh, McGregor," Calahan blubbered through tears, "our wonderful, wonderful, McGregor."

Chapter 18

When Franky, Squizzle and their rescuers got back to the forest just as the sun was dropping behind the horizon, Byron and The Team were waiting nervously on the edge of the lake. Upon witnessing the commotion, Poppy had flown home to alert The Team that the others were on their way.

The look on Byron and The Team's faces when the foursome burst through the thick brush and bound toward them across the tree-trunk was priceless. They couldn't wait to hear what happened. Thankfully, Byron and Rhys both seemed to have forgotten all about Franky and Squizzle's punishment.

Back at the cottage, McGregor had been lapping up all the old man and Harriet's attention and gratitude. Finally, he was back in their good graces. But though he was happy to be safe at home, he couldn't help but wonder when he'd get to see his new friends again.

Thankfully, the forest had no shortage of adventures in store.

About the Author

Russell Morris lives in Melbourne, Australia and is a father of three children. His imagination continually runs wild and has been accused many times of being a child in an adults body. "The inspiration for this book comes from being silly with my kids and not taking life too seriously."

9 781839 346477